VERMILLION
to
ONE

Vermillion to One: a crime poem

Copyright © 2022 Jim DeFilippi and BROWN FEDORA BOOKS

Printed in the United States by KDP

Portions of this poem have appeared in the novel ANNAH TORCH 2

Cover photo of K. L. Wallace by Jamie DeFilippi

ISBN: 9798818503981

10 9 8 7 6 5 4 3 2 1

Vermillion to One

a crime poem

Jim DeFilippi

To my pals and poets

First Canto: Snatch and Release

The Corner Boy

You gonna finish them fries?

Lemme tug on your coat a couple minutes here, I be buying…

Nah, so I'm no Tom Waits, no Bukowski for sure

Just another Brown Shoe, shrapnel-skulled, greasy blue-collar vet,

sort of a Del Reeves "Bummin' in a One Bum town" town bum

But still, I got us a story to tell

You could do worse than a quick sip'n'listen.

Don't kid yourself,

this'll be a Narragansett-fueled bonanza of stanzas

I'll smack my lips, be a placemat, tour guide, *Our Town* stage manager, Geek Chorus

Yeah, I said Geek, so buckle up, and lay em down

You got any questions, I'm here. Don't ask. Just keep sipping and listening

What you don't understand don't matter

Put down your bottle— use the coaster, Jerry the barkeep gets mad— and listen up.

So this thing starts off with an abduction— okay?

A snatch off a wet street, huh?

A girl— a woman,

Onna sidewalk one minute, then off it. Gone.

Her name signs in as…

~ ~ ~ ~

Ivy Torch

Hearing that *sforzondo* snap,

Feeling the leather of my *Manolo Blahniks* being lifted from the pavement,

a David Blaine levitation, but stagehand assisted

Then— thrown hard into the burnt-clay brick wall outside *Molly's Deli*,

backdrop to backstop, bone to stone. That snap, was it mine? Skeletal?

Bones that break easy, my curse, for always.

Jump cut:

My face and nose pressed hard into some blinding, reeking, leaking carpeting

A van, rattling, smoking, farting out used carbon like a formerly owned Toyota

Save all this up, Ivy— store it away somewhere in the synapses, for the cops, later on

Count the minutes they're driving me

Ascertain the miles, the turns left and right— any railroad stops, factory whistles?

Sounds. Register them. File to memory.

Highway or waterfront alleyway

Good god, sweet Jesus, what would Annah do?

Okay, but you shall not cry out

No cursing, no angry-confused, panicked complaints, not from this little muffin

Restraint shall be my re-strength

Sublimation my salvation. Please, dear god, allow us no whimpering here

Annah would not permit it, Daddy hated wussying too: "Buck it up, little lady."

Annah? God? Daddy? Heaven. Please?

My arms yanked hard behind me, wrists held together back there with shoulders
Shaking

A mutt-husky voice intoning...

~ ~ ~ ~

Cradle! Hey, Cradle, listen up! So gimme quick them twist-ties there,

Jerk-off, I told ya we needed um.

"You letting her wiggle, Mootz, *schmukus"*

Huh?

"She starts in wiggling like that, who knows the fug that ends up."

The twist-ties. Quick. You bring um or not?

"No. It's not twist-ties you mean anyway.

Them are the little shits you use to seal up bread with—

them little wire twirly twisties things. Them are..."

Okay, gimme some duck tape then. It's over there, give it here.

"Wrong again. It's *duct*. With a big duck-ass T at the end."

Duck? What?... what?... huh?... fug? What the fug? Fug, fug, fug. Fuck it.

"Don't let her wiggle, jeez-head. You keep on letting her wiggle like that, *doof*. Jesus."

She is... ahh, fug...

~ ~ ~ ~

Ivy Torch

So then, this abduction is being conducted by savages

Stooges

Monkeys with ropes and binders

No reason to panic, not yet

Just two *jamokes*

Simply must keep my bones and mind intact

Their un-synced, phrase-splintering dialogue

 just a butter-fried routine from an Orpheus Circuit vaudeville act

These two are not Leopold and Loeb.

I am being abducted by Lennie and Squiggy.

~ ~ ~ ~

Daddy

Rewind, 1980s:
A flip off a red, dusty, trusty tricycle
or sliding off a slippery rock unto hard pack
"Everything okay then, sweetie, you're all right?
Anything amiss? Let's make sure nothing's been compromised."

~ ~ ~ ~

The Corner Boy

So now, this abducted deducting one, she's got herself a sister, okay?

Annah the older

And tougher, huh? Lots tougher, stronger...

Another Torch, burning bright— but oblivious out there

in her fuggen woodlands beloved,

her forest primeval, uncluttered by specifics, engulfed by the general.

Since thirteen years old, blessed, cursed (they tell me) shrouded by:

a muscles-shriveling, scruples-bluring, dick-hardening beauty.

Body and face, a thin damning layer of flesh, wrapped over bone and being.

Annah abandoned the civilized world four years ago, no apology, explanations,

to go live in the six-point-one million untamed acres

of the Adirondack National Forest,

an ancient world of old-growth timber,

10,000 lakes slivered by 30,000 miles of river and stream.

She's an anomaly— is that the right word?

Crooked, twisted trees get ignored,

left to stand, thrive, to strengthen

While the straight, common wood is buzz-sawed into planks

sold to condo constructors in the city.

Her last campsite was burned to the ground by sadistic, stupid *mufus*,

hired by some much admired industrialist hotshot,

some psychopath who'd hunted her,

their deer rifles locked and loaded with vengeance,

bubbling out like spit spraying from between yellowed teeth.

Annah killed them.

With rock and hammer and a twist of the neck.
Killed every last one of them.

~ ~ ~ ~

Annah Torch

Atrocity is the moth of invention.
Finality its flame.

~ ~ ~ ~

Ivy Torch

My terrorized mind, slipping gears like this Toyota van stink-womb.

Rewind 1932:

The dry flood of the Great Depression submerging the country,

Hoover sagging into Roosevelt

Abductions springing up like dandelions across the green manicured lawns of millionaires

Bankers, wankers, body-shankers, not just kids being napped—

The Lindberg baby. With that other lung-sucking wound of Hoover—

J. Edgar

mashing his publicity-sniffing snout into any case promising ink,

apprehension and rescue displaced by credit and publicity

The baby murdered. Maybe dropped to its death from a home-made wooden ladder.

Will I be murdered too?

A Fatty Arbuckle defenestration unto my own eradication?

Was it a Bruno? Bruno Hopman?

Hauptman. Something like that. Hauptman.

If it was a German madman killed your son, Charles, why love Nazis so much?

Gear up, Ivy, this is now, girl, not Nazi time, but now,

with just a couple of this-century *jamokes.*

If my hands could loosen, I'd slap my own face into

the harsh practicality of my present situation

Annah, where are you?

~ ~ ~ ~

The Corner Boy

Still with me here, jazz-bo? So why this snatch, you're asking me?

Shad-ap, just keep sipping

Michael Corleone: "Never ask me about my business, Kay.

All right, just this once. One time."

All right, poetry lovers, just this once:

Ivy is a scientist– holding a measly bank account and brain-sacks full of cerebral brawn

Good, not evil brawn. No Eva Braun.

There is a ransom to be demanded here, but not in sheckles, not with *grooble*

But a Nazi's ransom to be paid off with insight. With knowledge.

With notes

coded in her old grammar school notebook, cover speckled with black and white splotches

That's what these *jambonies* are after

That notebook, with her name printed across the front cover, the proud name...

~ ~ ~ ~

Ivy Torch

How many days of holding is it now? Three, could it be? Maybe more?

I tried counting the suns from between the cracks of the steel door

How many days of torture, extraction, mutilation, and rape?

Days of coma and Oxford comma

My salvation has been that coin, that nickel

Gray, dulled by age, imbedded into the fake barn-board paneling across this

inner-sanctumed room

Protecting my sanity,

Demanding my focus,

Preserving my purity,

Strengthening my resolve, lifting me from this obscenity of captivity

A U.S. minted swirling kaleidoscope, brown smudges mixing into reflecting puddles

A kaleidoscope, a calliope, twisting onto its side now, and rolling itself towards me

A growling Kenworth semi

As they come again with their pliers and swollen cocks,

The surface of my coin blurs itself,

misshapen by my tears, morphing into a Dali clock

I continue to resist.

Now the coin is balanced on my silk-haired fingers

a ballerina flipping across my knuckle tops,

Pinky to forefinger, back and forth, a caged tiger

I am a gambler, a card-shark, Michelle Obama, Jim Valvano, I am my sister— Annah.

Surrender is for pussies.

~ ~ ~ ~

You can either spit or swallow, lil sweet chicken, don't matter to me

If it's teardrops or just some wet jizz, we don't care,

it ain't *my* wet no more, belongs to you

So enjoy

That there what you just got's called a Cuban Sandwich, sweetie,

You like it?

I think ya gave me a blood pressure headache from all the fuggin, but that's okay

You ready to spill your fried beans now for us, chicken?

Your notes?

Or else it can be back to Cuba for ya, if you want

Back-door bumpin front-hatch humpin

I got it in my sack a repeat performance

You too, Cradle, you got it in ya, huh?

You know, doll, it's not you bein brave any more

Just stubborn and fuggen stupid is all it is.

~ ~ ~ ~

Drink up, pal.

Ivy, my heart goes off to you.

While we're waiting for her deliverance, lemme introduce Ivy's angry antagonies

(Is that the word? Spell Check says No, but I can't find it)

Anyway this merry band of kidnapping miscreants comprised of...

Top of the pyramid:

a Mr. Zeigfried Adamsavage

South African import. Both front pockets stuffed with racism

Managed to sneak his polluted psyche past Customs

onto our pure white American countryside

Ming the Merciless with a black poker chip on each pasty-skinned shoulder

Next, in descending order:

Mother Harpo. Fifty-three year old female (but not feminine) motorcycle gangbanger

Twin Happy Face tats on her alveoli

Harpo Marx doubleganger (Is that the word? It's Krout-speak?)

Hired out to Adamsavage to do his wet work for him

She understands this boss to be delusional, psychotic, but he pays well

Brought along her two subordinate stooges (have you met?) who are:

#1 Big Mootz: Née Angelo Mozzella

A fat, fatty lover of cheese, bugs, and resistant pussy

Loyal to Mother, puts nothing above her.

#2 Robin "The Cradle" Schmertz,

convicted child molester, sewer level parasite.

That's it.

~ ~ ~ ~

Ziegfried Adamsavage

This great country of yours,

A blubber backed, beached whale, flopping,

suffocating on the sands of your Coney Island

This lumbering, slumbering, stupid, magnificent America of yours

Watered by years of myth-thickened blood, misdirected love

Unanswered Capote prayers.

Ask: Where are the forces brute, the repeater rifles, the Gatling guns?

A-bombs denuding, then skinning Hiroshima?

"We had to kill the village to save it," yeah?

Nazi policy *Akton T4*, ten out of a thousand Germans christened as *Unworthy of Life*

Unfit to Live. Processed to be euthanized

The mentally challenged, the poor, sick, old, Jews 'n' gypsies, scrub them all off

Your Lindbergh, Henry Ford, they saw the light

Kaffers strolling the streets like certified citizens.

This America, this whole world, could be a beautiful, bleached and blanched garden
Yeah?

Ich bin ein Berliner.

I am a simple gardener— constant, a landscaper of humanity,

Plucking weeds

And the *kaffers* are the weeds, yeah?

Kaffers, we call them, yeah?

Kaffers. Law breakers, shank shakers, shit-fakers

clipper-shipped over here from my home continent— chained up, submissive,
emitting poverty,

19

grief, cotton pickers, whining, rape, drugs.

Okay then, maybe a few singers, tap dancers, a horn player, cool jazz, Satchmo

My Pappy saw him once in Johannesburg– blowing lips and inflating cheeks for the U.N.

Loved him *St. James Infirmary*.

So, it's Satch and that sperm-hose who fathered the Jackson Five, but who else?

You're hearing me then, Mother Harpo, you are, yeah?

Just have your boys elicit the notebook, that's all I am asking.

~ ~ ~ ~

Mother Harpo

Zeigfried Adamsavage is an imbecile, a madman, a lunatic,

the worst kind too, the kind's got money

I'm just here to relieve him a portion of it

with my chopper gang, know in town as the Polo Rodeo

Just me and Mootz and the Cradle

we do what we're paid to, that's all,

So if it means torturing up some pretty little du-da like...

~ ~ ~ ~

Ivy Torch

My mental spools, unwinding into a thick and captured darkness...

At eight years old, down at the Frog Pond, catching transmogrifying polliwogs

a slippery flip into the muddy water,

Annah ruined her shoes in my rescue.

"Don't tell Dad, we weren't supposed to even be there."

At eleven, Jones Beach,

Dad tells us the Robert Moses story, goes to sleep on the sand, straw hat across his face

A rip tide grabs me, whisked from chest-high to Can't Touch Bottom

"Annah, I need..."

My sister frog-kicks us back in

Teenager, dallying with some boy— was it Kevin Sadler?

Giggling, kissing, warning each other

nervous fingers rubbing across forbidden parts

my boot jammed into the cleave of Split Rock. Won't budge.

Jokes about amputation.

"You have to go get my sister."

But now, now and here, the steel door stays bolted, the coin of my salvation blurring

Annah isn't coming for me

Nobody is

Only this eternal cesspool of debasement and danger

awaits me.

~ ~ ~ ~

So, Annah, she's oblivious, right, ya understand?

She's out there among her pine trees, swimming naked every morning

Her callipygian charms (that's the word, "callipygian," is it? Means "sweet ass"?)

revealed only to the birds. The geese

The blackbirds skimming wingtips across the water surface

Turkey vultures perching on the branches by the shore

tracking her with dark, lust-flooded eyes.

Annah: Oblivious, obsessed, dedicated, focused

Endless trips stroked back and forth across the rippling surface of Robert's Pond

Breathe, stroke, kick, breath, stroke, kick...

Leaving that magnificent body fatigued, tender to the touch

After that— the biking

Riding a previously stolen J.C. Higgins

that the Weasel picked up for her at police auction. Five bucks.

Neck stiff from hours of holding the head upright,

Just glancing down to avoid rocks, gullies, logs

Then: R.O.B.: Run Off the Bike.

Deer-like, soft, silent, poetic, hooves barely touching the ground—

boots crunching the gravel like a meat grinder

Breathing, working like a steam engine

Toenails blackened with blood blisters

bubbling there beneath the surface.

~ ~ ~ ~

Annah Torch

In training to run a solitary Ironman,
One woman. No competition,
except what I bring

~ ~ ~ ~

The Corner Boy

Yeah, a solitary competitor. Annah vs Annah

Hermit vs. the same hermit

Her only neighbor in the Woods, her sole friend—

The black man, Hurricane Abel

offering some aid, assistance,

maybe mildly nodded encouragement

but little else.

Now our girl is juggling,

gliding, guiding softball sized rocks arching through the air,

hoping to surpass twelve,

The magic number of Alan Šulc of the Czech Republic

And three dimensional chess

Reconstructing matches in her mind,

Kasparov vs. Topalov—1999 Rotlewi vs. Rubenstein— 1907

But with width, breath, *and* depth.

Ironman Tri, Michelle Obama, juggling, chess,

each teaching Annah to test her limits,

although she may have not have any to test.

All the time, oblivious to her sweet sister's torrid trials

Annah testing her own limits, limits that might not even exist.

While the madman— Zeigfried Adamsavage— along with Mother Harpo and her Polo Rodeo,

go about proving that theory wrong.

~ ~ ~ ~

I'm ready.
It's "Uncle."
I'm telling you, I say, "Uncle," I'm done for.

"Listen, sweet cakes, nobody ain't walkin through that door to save your sweet ass,
so you might just as well…"

I told you, I'm ready. I'm done. Finished. I'm yours.

With *schmukes* like you two, Stockholm is simply a city, not a syndrome.
Go get your boss. Tell him I've been caved.
All *sangfroid* dilutes through time and plasma.

My notes are at the The First Federal Bank of Albany.
The First Federal Bank of Albany.

~ ~ ~ ~

Yup, Bank of Albany

Still with me? Holding on? Scraping mug bottom? Need a refill?

The bank's Second Head Teller is

a spindly-moving young doe,

face powdered pale as a whitetail deer

running from a rifle shot,

released from her cage,

her plastic chest-plate labeling her as "Nance,"

not Nancy

Nance is leading Ivy out of the Albany Safe Deposit Box Room.

~ ~ ~ ~

Ivy Torch

The room being the same size as held my captivity
but everything is different outside those walls.

Has the world changed,
or have I?

~ ~ ~ ~

Nance the Teller

I have been caged at this bank for two, almost three years now
Me and all the girls not even allowed to pace in circus captivity behind our steel bars
So we enjoy any release, any assignment to let the caged bird sing—
coffee, Staples for supplies, *The Golden Wok* to bring back lunch
I'm pleased to escort this client, this nervous, messed-up, horror-eyed woman
to her box in the Safety Deposit area
where she removes a scuffed, soft-sided, orange-aged, calfskin briefcase,
peppered with buckles, zippers, pockets and flaps,
stuffed to bulging with crinkled papers, binders, notebooks.

Wow— then— but she stops, glances about,
presses the case into the front of my Bean Classic Funnelneck Pullover, the tan one

"Take this, please, start running down that hallway, I'll come back for it later."

~ ~ ~ ~

Ivy Torch

My mind has been left soggy,
soiling the floor, back at the torture chamber
but it can still form occasional thoughts, unveil occasional plans—
of escape.
Maybe not like I could before, but still with quick little bubbles of explosion.

"I said take it, please, run..."

~ ~ ~ ~

Big Mootz

Me and the Cradle, we're standin there, watchin our chicken—

Holy Christ,

all of a sudden she's splittin

she goes one way, the clerk girl holdin onto the briefcase goin the other way

Wadda ya want from me?

The thing Mother wants, demands, for Adamsavage— it's the briefcase

holdin the notes

We gotta come back with that at least, and with her too,

or we're roadkill

But Christ, there's *two* women, they're both goin their separate ways,

we gotta bring um both back, chick'n'notes— so now what?

Wadda ya want from me?

The Cradle's askin, as if I know,

"Mootz, wadda we do? Mootz, wadda we gonna..."

Cradle, listen, there's two of us, right? You and me? That makes two

and there's two of them

There's the one widda notes, and the chicken, so we just split...

~ ~ ~ ~

Ivy Torch

Standing in the bank lobby, I consider syntax:
"He *has* a gun"?
No. Too formal. Unemotional. Too conventional, too proper.
So then, it's the colloquial:
"He got a gun, he got a gun!"
Pointing at the two stupid troglodyte thugs,
my own hand formed into a pistol grip and muzzle
as if to show the crowd what a gun looks like.

And the lobby screams itself alive with echos.

~ ~ ~ ~

Madge, Delores, and Little Delores,
all disappear like Wack-a-Moles below their cage holes.
The new girl at drive-by drops to her knees,
crawling across tile, begging her God and the two goons for mercy.
"Please, please, sir, I'm an aunt, I got cousins..."

~ ~ ~ ~

Ivy Torch

Calm yourself. Be an Annah.
Walk to the electronic doors
they sweep themselves open at my regal approach
I hustle my calm path through their archway,
turn right, down the sidewalk, away from the bank,
toward some semblance of emotional, physical freedom
A freedom I can only hope will be more than temporary

~ ~ ~ ~

The Corner Boy

Look, I fully intested to be just a decent docent here,

a prop master in all of this.

Narrator, not instigator, of any action

Not looking to get myself onto centerstage at all, see?

But it was me who found the little mazzie, Ivy,

flop-floundering out there on the concrete street,

A slag Dumpster for her head pillow,

Chanticleering something about Joe DiMaggio

It was me brought her to the Weasel.

Some background:

By profession, I am a top-flight panhandler here in White Leung, New York

Work these dream streets six days a week,

On Tuesdays, the Weasel brings me into Albany

corner where Slingerland meets Bogart

where I consistently double my stay-at-home week's take-in

The Weasel, he's okay

What I am to the cracked alleys of this town,

Howard J. Wyzell Esq. is to its hollowed chambers

So I recognized the delirious Ivy, know her sister used to do Weasel work,

before heading off into the Woods to live like Goldilocks with tits

So I brung her to him

A relay throw from the outfield to Big Sister's mitt— her hut.

~ ~ ~ ~

Ivy Torch

My delirium has swirled off onto the sides of my sight
Where is this I am? Here.

"Here" is a drafty, crude, pile of sticks,
amidst an intimidating forest of angry trees and cold stones
The walls of this room— can I call it a room?— just sloppy bundles of twigs
pockmarked by gaping holes, loose twines, leaves,
handfuls of pine-needle randomly stuffed between the branches
The smell of woodsmoke,
hints of decay, mold
the burlap raw wool blanket unable to keep out the wet freeze
rocks, pebbles, hard and unforgiving, pressing into my back.
The place could be destroyed by a subtle gust of wind

But none of it matters, because leaning above my pain-throbbing body,
is my Annah. My sister.
A concerned look of love splayed across her beautiful face
She strokes my forehead, touches my hair,
the confusion, not the cold, causing my body to shiver.

I am with Annah. She shall exorcise my madness.
I ask, "Did DiMaggio get his hit?"

~ ~ ~ ~

Lie back, Ivy. Lips together, teeth apart. Breathe.

You're safe now, girl. Safe.

It's me.

Try not to think.

~ ~ ~ ~

Annah, did my bones get any cracks in them?

I have been corroded, haven't I? Corrupted

I am finding myself unable to grasp any... thoughts, feelings, anything

My synapses are clogged. Snapped into uselessness.

Daddy told us Hemingway killed himself when the words wouldn't come, remember?

Where is Daddy?

Really? No. Gone? How long ago?

Who brought me here?

So it's Thursday? You mean now? What Thursday is that?

Did DiMaggio get his hit?

~ ~ ~ ~

The Corner Boy

Okay, so to recap:
So, Zeigfried's lost hold of his lady scientist,
who's trying to reclaim her damaged mind
out there in her sister's beloved Woodlot,
but at least he's got her notebook.
It's lying right there on his desktop
right beside his iced Orange Crush
holding the formula to DamAx-30(af)
The serum that Dr. Ivy uncovered in her search for pandemic solution
A pathogen targeting the black race (af = African),
Zeigfried's yellow sickle cell road to genocide.

Trouble is— these notes are useless to him,
cause they're all written in something called...

~ ~ ~ ~

Timothy Roy Tides

Nüshu– The Script of Women
Secretive, gentle, feminine
Threadlike in its subtlety, woven into fabric, onto stray pieces of cloth,
embroidered within the wing of a fan
aesthetically beautiful, self-enclosed communication of Tenth Century women,
Jaingyong County, Human province, south China
So now, finally, women– chained to illiteracy for centuries,
subjugated into invisibility–
can write.
Logographic, omnipotent in its simplicity,
Sub-rosa, horizontal– like a woman's pure form reclining upon a carpet

"When standing beside a sister, one feels no despair."

A text delivered woman to woman– ensconced, enclosed,
protected from the dictatorship of the male Qing Dynasty,
They find themselves suddenly condemned to illiteracy.

These are the notes of Ivy Torch.

~ ~ ~ ~

I strive for cognizance, for some goddamn logical description
but what is all this shit anyway?
Page upon page of gibberish twaddle
Chink writing, in all probability
Those two flee-eaten *moegoes* of yours, Mother,
with their boneys leaking gas and fumes,
their brains leaking cognitive thought,
they both leave here with our *kont* in tow,
to return holding only these useless shit-sheets of hieroglyph,
lines going up and down, like a hard-on
Brain-stalled

But *mia cooples*, I suppose, yeah? Is it not?
Twas I, after all, ascertained those two blokes made the sundae,
raped the lassie into submission,
so I allowed them to put the cherry on top, accompany her to the bank.
(Where some men have conscience, or intellect, those two have airbags)
So, all right, to decipher, that's *bakgat*– should not present a problem then, yeah?
Ja, eventually,
B.L.S. Black Lives Splatter.
Our task may be time sensitive, with a closing shelf life, but the Internet is not
The deciphering lies there before us, cloaked in its scratches of ink and pixel
Darwin, eugenics, DamAx, shall prevail, yeah?
Our Bubonic Plague shall eventually metastasize as planned
with proper research, and science.

Google wankers, coding in their mammy's basement

our answer shall be found.

To float like milkweed through the air of this bastardized world— purifying,
regenerating

Twas volcanic ash killed the dinosaurs. The ash shall be *us*, this time.

Kill the lizards, Mother, crack the code, gain control of the DamAx

Destroy all black lizards.

~ ~ ~ ~

I first comma da Woods, uma man all a-busted up

Drugs n shit

Nobody want me but the cops

Nobody lookin' out fa me but da devil

Annah, she hep me build my camp

"Long as it sits not too close to mine."

She hep me out

Gimme my life back

Now she be tryin' do the same wit da lil girl

looks like her

Sisters. In sorry shape though

Talkin', coughin', makin' no sense a-tall.

She gonna be a lot tougher juke-job den I ever was.

~ ~ ~ ~

#1: "Find a stand-alone letter, an A or I, maybe O."

No, these symbols look like the menu

at Ching Lee's House of Finely Chopped Chop Suey

#2: "Look for what comes after the punctuation— period, comma, especially the apostrophe."

No, you see see any colons here? Semi-colons? Colonoscopies are useless

#3: "Keep a fresh, sharp eye on the pattern used on the keyboard."

No QWERTY, just a stubby pencil and a couple notebooks

w/ a splotched b&w cover

#4: "Forget the square cipher, it's Julius Caesar."

Before the Brute they called *Et 2* turned him into a pin cushion, he was coding—

lining up letters, shifting them steps to the right, left.

 #5: "Start by identifying the code being used"

Number substitution? No. Keyboard code? Of course not.

So...

I had pointed all this out to Ivy. Codes are made to be broken.

So substitute the word "language"

Not Mandarin, Putonghua, Min, Gan, Wu

Find an alphabet endangered— unknown, unused

Use *Nüshu.*

With it, you'll start splashing yourself with gravy.

~ ~ ~ ~ ~

God damn it, we don't *have* any *schoepit* fucking letters here, now do we, yeah?

Morons and misfits, you may step down

I am appointing myself Project Manager, Prime Minister

Mootz, go back to watching bugs fight, or playing with your paperclips

whatever it is you do for fun.

Mother, Cradle, ease back.

Legwork replaces leg breaking— scholarship—

no knuckle-busters need apply

What we need— worming nerds wearing reading glasses

hunched over their keyboards and computer screens,

swayed backs, tired eyes, smart phoning smart friends for directional signals,

Solve this riddle named *Nüshu* (its name yet unknown to me)

White-collared scholars, scratch pads, advanced degrees, brains,

No motorcycle nightmares of dropping jaws, clouded-over eyes

stranded in a corn maze of false gods,

The Blessed Trinity of Pixels, Electrons, and Holy Ghostly images

Faculty offices, degrees on the walls, gowned photographs on the desk

"Yes, I think we read at Cambridge together— Harvard, Stanford— did we not?"

"Professor, take a look at these photostats. Any idea what it means, Doctor?"

Answers not found in Google-topia, or universities,

within pentagram Pentagon walls,

or in research labs funded by corporations packing federal grants.

Rather, infused within the brain of some ordinary bloke, working in his basement,

Mom knows he's a genius, nobody else

Neighbors whistle, circle their skulls, and whisper "Looney Tunes" as he strolls by

head in the clouds– they cumulous or semi-cumulous?
Back to the drawing and quartering board

Find such a guy
Release the hounds

~ ~ ~ ~

In the thinly layered, tightly focused sliver of the world I inhabit,

I am considered the leading independently funded/supported expert

in the field of Endangered Alphabets.

Originally a proud Brit,

educated at the Worcester Royal Grammar School, Pembroke College at Oxford,

Majoring in pickled onions and good cheddar,

I came to this country intending to achieve consummate acclaim

as a writer

or maybe a tennis champion,

perhaps a flamenco guitarist, the superstar mid-wicket of a cricket team,

before discovering and settling upon my true calling and proudest creation:

The Endangered Alphabet Permanent Symposium.

So now… Partially contented with my life, yet still partially frustrated,

I sit in the basement laboratory of the home I share with my domestic partner of three years,

a preschool teacher off teaching the rudimentary signs of the English language

I have carved the wooden face of a clock displaying its numerals in the *Adlam* symbol system

My fingers, especially the thumbs, are sore, weakened from the exertion

I am resting them

to practice a Paul Siebel song on my Takamine P3DC twelve-string acoustic-electric guitar

flexing and un-flexing, hoping not to soak them in warm salt water

soaking weakens the muscles,

turns the fingertip calluses softer, more painful to the fret press.

My eyes are closed,

my head resting on the recliner,
quietly humming the melody of the song to be attempted, maybe *Bride 1945*
as the doorbell rings upstairs
The Bells of Rhymney

These Bells will sound out my funereal chime.
~ ~ ~ ~

Um no Fuller Brush Man

Jehosephat Witness, Publicans Clearing House,

Sellin solar panels some shit. None a that.

This creep knows that, lets me in anyhow,

half shit-scared/half just bein polite

half bored, kinda interested in what I be pushin

Me there smellin like crank case oil, givin off some phony name

"It that Jewish?"

Wadda fuck, Jewish?

I tell him I got no business card, ask for a glass of water, upstairs,

he calls back down, "Ya want ice in dat?"

What am I, Princess Diana?

He musters up the courage, asks me what um doin here, why is it I cum

So I use his name, show him the skinny broad's scratch-writing on my iPad

He gets happy— I'm here cause he's some expert

What's this guy, talkin like a fairy queen, wearin a scarf around his pencil neck?

When I twist the scarf hard, his eyes gettin bigger, like two donut Munchkins

He's choke-spittin out three fax for me:

1.   He's the one led the chicken to her code— it's chink writing all right

2.   But he don't know which one code it is, she's the only one knows that

3.   Chicken's got a sister lives out in the Woods

All this I learn before goin upstairs, phonin up Mother, then comin back down

Shootin him in the mouth.

Guy's big front teeth cracklin like popcorn.

~ ~ ~ ~

Third Canto: Vermillion Ways to Die

Counselor Wyzell— Wyzell, is it? Do I pronounce the surname correctly?

Pleasure

Thank you for the opportunity

We are two men conflicted by scheduling, so I shall be brief

I have been attempting to set up a business consort with one Miss Ivy Torch

Simply in order to cover some technical procedures. With her.

Chemical components, production methods, such elements,

you understand

As do I— understand that is— that this Miss Torch's sister, one Annah,

is a previous employee of yours

who has cloaked herself indisposed (as I have ascertained through local folklore)

but to whom you still have access, yeah?

The only one who does, I believe

Only you

And she, Annah, in turn, might well possess accessibility to my quarry— sister Ivy

Follow?

Thus, I request of you that you use your social linkage

to explain to Miss Torch, to both sisters actually,

that until we are able to sit down and communicate together— Miss Ivy and I—

What shall occur is this—

On a extremely regular basis—

Say, each and every three days, four tops—

(Oh, "The Four Tops," do you know them?

A marvelous vocal group, of rhythm and blues, I believe you would say,

R. and B.)

— that until that meeting can be arranged and brought to fruition,
one local negress per time-period

Shall be eradicated.

~ ~ ~ ~

Mother Harpo

Stoop shouldered, snail-curled, pseudo-hunchbacked,

dragging a dead body across a cornfield

Its black skin bleached out by death to a tint glowing white in the moonlight

Mouth hanging open, silent, screaming,

Eyes screaming too— forty-five minutes ago

The Great Mandela, spinning until a head-shot of potassium chloride

ground things to a halt. A dead stop.

The throat having suffered a thousand career-demanded internal debasements,

now released from servitude by a butcher knife

Brown bangs dangling across the forehead, colorizing the monochromatic,

brown hair stretching down to the waist,

dead brown-browed brown eyes, lacquered with goos of smeared paint,

staring out at an eternity which once held promise

A silver blade-truncated life

dabs of that silver paint the face— a nose ring, a wire infinity sign ear-ring

angling from an ear pocketed with blood.

And the monster drags the body.

Lips hinting a smear of a lavender cosmetic,

Teeth white, cracked and missing, prior to tonight's savagery

Sloppy inked tattoos of

a southwestern landscape— Arizona or New Mexico, Saguaro cacti and mountains

upper chest showing a script almost biblical:

Ornate twisting letters— all capitals— from some other language, maybe Spanish

(not *Nüshu*)

"*Yo tu quan...*" its continuation covered by lengths of brown hair, by the position of the body, by the shadows in the moon light

The upper arm manly, covered with black hair, muscled by unsuccessful strains of survival

The clothing professional— a stained dung colored t-shirt over black bra straps,

 A tight aqua-colored skirt, barely covering the business section of the body...

~ ~ ~ ~

Mother Harpo, she's going on for too damn long here, don't ya think?
Enjoying herself too god-damn much with the human atrocity of it all

Hey, you want something from the back?
A burger maybe?
Jerry makes a meat pie like Aladdin.

~ ~ ~ ~

Mother Harpo

Am I killing my mother each time I tug that blade across some whorey throat?

Fuck Freud, I'm just taking out the garbage

A fifty-bucks service fee?

For what? For that?

Wait a second, lemme see if I got a fifty here in my sheath

Don't you run away, sweetheart.

~ ~ ~ ~

You able to keep everything down?

With all this torment coming up, going down?

I hope so.

How bout some jukebox music?

What'll it be for ya? Maybe Beach Boys?

~ ~ ~ ~

Mother Harpo

The whore's shirt stretched over a belly seeming to swell with life, even in death

Maybe a child nestled in there? A prosecutorial charge of *double* Homicide One
Premeditated?

The unfortunate mama, plus her fetus of misfortune?

The dead whore's legs—

blacker than the dirt and dead grass they're being dragged across

a blackboard jumble

The "Come to mama" stockings

luring the farm boys from under the Sandburg street lamps

both feet swollen, pointing opposite directions.

The body is drugged into a sideboard shack

emanating the size and smell of an outhouse,

originally erected for machine and tool storage.

The floorboards are gray, splintered with shards of broken bottles

A crudely hammered shelf manages to hang onto the back wall

The hunchback waves one hand in the air

Her fist taps a thin chain hanging from a single light bulb

The chain is tugged, the bulb pops on, and— ironically,

the room is brightened, enlightened with a blinding 100-watt explosion

The body is splayed out across the dirt floor

then pressed flat.

She is Degas, preparing an empty canvas for artistry

A can of *Benjamin Moore Flat Oil-Based Exterior House Paint*

Its color labeled "Vermillion Blend" a sample smear thumb-smudged below the label

The murderer uses a flat-edge screwdriver to open the can,
only after violently shaking exactly one hundred times
The hunchback counts aloud as her muscled arms shake
3/4 an inch of paint poured into the pan
A newly unwrapped roller slips into its Zorro wire handle
Mother Harpo dips the roller, rolls the wheel across the tray,
then, gently, gently across the body of the dead prostitute.

~ ~ ~ ~

Hell, I thought that part about Mother and the tramp she stamped
was stretched out far too long
Don't ya think? I'll try to do better. After all, we gotta beat "Last Call."

Okay, now, two cops:
Leo Protski, Special Investigator for the D. A.'s office,
and Simon L. Gumm, Head of Major Crimes, White Leunge, New York, P.D.
(a one-man department)
The two of them've been bantering,
trading smack talk at crime scenes for years, decades
Tossing out gags like antiseptics
Trying to hang onto some protective distance
While, same time, to their sanity.

Gumm is short, round, shaped like the single clasp of a pair of handcuffs
Protski, tall and thin— a patrolman's billy club
Both smart cops, not brilliant, intelligent, capable— able to think while
chewing gun with the front of their government-issue dentures
Each holding onto a couple handful shards of a busted moral code
Gumm, pockets stuffed with pencil-struck racing forms and crumpled-up loser stubs
Protski packing a horny bitterness toward his ex-wife
Both working under the yoke and auspices of District Attorney Sarah T. Guffleberg
(Never call her "Goofy" to her face)
A strange, power-lusting woman— always playing off-stage, but stage managing,
A woman comprised entirely of political aspiration

built upon the successful prosecution of high profile "Red Ball" cases

She won't like this "Killing whores, painting the cadavers" crap,

until it can get successfully prosecuted.

She tells Gumm to use the Voice Memo on his phone, instead of his old Columbo notebook.

"My own voice talking back to me on my telephone won't ever know as much as I do."

~ ~ ~ ~

So I tell her, I say to her, I say…

"Say what? What you say?"

My own voice talking back to me on my telephone won't ever know as much as I do.

"Uh-huh. So look here, he's been using a roller again. Stains across this dead vic."

Took Michelangelo six years, the Sistine Chapel ceiling.

"What?"
Could've finished in a morning, he used a roller. Like this one.

"Glad you're keeping it light, pard, you're a not-so-young Henny Youngman,

the vic's mom would appreciate."

Ya see the spots he missed? Under the breasts there, the hip? Used a roller.

"Columbo."

Roller's designed n built to do flat. No contours.

 "This body's not flat. She got all the right curves. She could use another coat."

Yeah, this gal had some contours on her. Effective for the trade.

"Base coat— mascara, lipstick, body ink— prison-pressed or self-administered."

So, our vic started her evening painted with cosmetics, luring in the horny, now she's
dead.

"Painted with latex, luring us crime boys to go out and find who killed her."

Which we are tracking. How many hardware stores, paint places, can there be?

"Looks like maybe she once was somebody with a couple shares of a future, no?"

When will they ever learn?

"Pete Seeger. Where have all the street flowers gone? Long time murdered."

Pete? Nah. Peter, Paul and Mary, maybe? Lime Lighters?

"I'll hum you a few bars."

No, don't do that. We'll get him. The whole thing is savage cleavage.

"When will they ever burn?"

Kingston Trio. They won't ever burn, not unless we catch 'em first.

"And unless Goofy thinks it's a Red Ball— indictable. And winnable."

And print worthy.

~ ~ ~ ~

Ivy Torch

My thoughts remain scattered
Splattered
Stained with pools and puddles of licorice-black waters
Deluding logic
Denuding reason
Drenching my world in incomprehensible sludge.

For brief moments "I can see clearly now, the clouds are gone"
My vision sharp inside a stilled and silent snow-globe
"I see no obstacles in my way"
The pretty little Christmas village is mine
This hut where Annah cares for me, is clear to me. Mine. Surrounds me.
It is now.
It is me.
Not 1941, before I was born.
I am not drowning in anachronism,
asking the wind if the Clipper got his hit.

Me. Now. Hanging on. Struggling my way back into the lineup.
My bat as potent as Dam-Ax30
But then the black waters return, swirling in from stage-left and stage-right,
Snow clouds angry at the sun,
Clashing, crashing together at center stage
"And if I have to go on living without Elvis,
then they can bring the curtain down."

(Daddy would play his old vinyls for us.)
Is my mind mix-metaphoring, whoring itself
into a total, everlasting smear of chaos?

~ ~ ~ ~

Stands behind the sisters without words
Trying to study the confusion
Understanding none of it
Only that his Annah is upset

And she is his friend.

~ ~ ~ ~

Ivy Torch

Annah is my sister, my friend,

she has always been handmaiden unto me

"Ivy, what they did to you was wrong.

Was. It's over.

Time and we together will make it right."

My blessed Angel Gabriella, my Guardian Angel, my Annah,

who, along with her faithful black Indian companion...

(Daddy had all the old Lone Rangers on tape,

We three would watch with soda and Orville Redenbacher)

Along with her faithful black Indian companion,

Who calls her...what?... Kemo?... Kemo what?

Kemo... Sabe?

Kemo... therapy?

"Ivy, we need help, I can get the Weasel to..."

No, no, keep it just you and I, Annah, we-us and the gentle hurricane

Your friend over here. We three. I'll get better.

I sense that Annah wants more than assistance,

she wants retribution.

Those who have caused this in me.

She wants to grab hold of Daddy's Hammer,

And go forth in fury.

No, Annah. No more violence. And no law.

69

I'll be fine. Just *fiiiii-ne.*
We just need some extra time, that's all.

Say hey, Willy Mays, did DiMaggio get his hit today?

~ ~ ~ ~

Mother Harpo

The hunchbacked creature has returned home
The front of her blue surgery scrubs stained with vermillion
Her face melted by encroaching morality
into a dripping plate of skin and tears
Mountains of remorse to be overcome, boat loads of regret to pilot through,
coal bins of blackened guilt and self-loathing to wash clean
This one was a mulatto girl with purple tats and silver nipple rings
To be stashed in an abandoned talc mine, out west of White Leunge,
its dirt walls showing whirls of white mineral, mixing with the red
and darkened flesh.

~ ~ ~ ~

Mother is bein' attended to by her apostles now.

We strip off her used-up clothes— the scrubs, the baggy jeans,

the red-stained bra and panties

to be launched into the washer-dryer,

I like *Premium Laundry Detergent Packs*,

along with *Snuggle* dryer sheets.

We take her into the shitter,

there we lower her tired, flattened ass onto the plastic toilet seat

then over to in-fronta the sink

Lay her head backwards

Let the warm water and sweet shampoo wash away the staining

Take her by both arms,

bring her to bed.

Flop her onto the mattress, she's callin' out for assistance from God

We two loyal ones have dressed her in her jamas,

the ones with the Charlie's Angels logos, their cotton red like cadaver paint

We lay her down— gentle, gentle,

cover her with some comfort and a comforter

tuck her in around her edges, like a baby.

She will always be our mother.

To us, she is forever our Mother Harpo.

~ ~ ~ ~

Murders for profit and joy, money to be handed over by the Savage Adam

Any subsequent painting of the cadavers is for her own amusement

Her victims are never "bodies" or "corpses"

They are cadavers.

Clinical, formal.

The money is practical, but the painting ritualistic,

with thoughts of high priests, formal gowns, tradition and ceremony.

Bestowing unto God what is His/Hers

Killing for the Savage money, but painting with compassion.

~ ~ ~ ~

and Mootz are in the cellar of the Cradle's brother's house,

painting a corpse

by Mother's direction,

her fetish by extension

Dirt floor, mossy stone walls,

a seventy-five Watt bulb hanging from a wire

in the deadened center of a split-log ceiling,

flashing a hard white light onto the once black/now white face of

Gina Fay Morgalis. Street name Bummy, or Bum,

bludgeoned, then knifed to death.

The Cradle laughs.

A little undertaker make-up please, maestro.

"Get up there around her eyes, like she's wearin' mistletoe."

Huh?

"Mistletoe. The black stuff hoes wear, hard-on, get up there around them eyes."

Mascara.

"Splash it on. Mother'll like that. Maybe we mush some in her cunk too, you think?"

I'm gonna need a stiffer brush.

~ ~ ~ ~

This kill.

The third in a three-legged stool of ignorance, loyalty, and moral rancidity,

began when the Cradle picked up a hooker just stumbled off the curb of Rancon Street,

bending over to retie the strings of her knee-high slut boot

Fee as advertised: a cool fifty

Mootz, hiding in the trunk of the Pontiac Bonneville,

hit suddenly with a smothering bout of claustrophobia,

began pounding on the tin from inside

The Cradle goes around to release his sweating and swearing partner,

apologizing to the whore for any delay,

Who is still expecting nothing more than some sweaty grunting and her fifty

But Mootz, trying to lift his three hundred pounds from the trunk,

slams his head. Hard.

The hoe questions this inconsistency:

"Why you got some fat guy gettin' out of your trunk for anyway?"

Mootz taps plump fingertips to his skull,

see his own blood— not somebody else's, as planned—

mixing with migraine-strength pain.

Enraged, he attacks,

using a greased and oiled Harley Davidson bike chain

with which he had previously been sharing trunk space

And the hunting knife.

The painting completed now,

The two dumb men pleased,

The corpse splashed with oil-based exterior
They sit and admire their work,
Sharing a bowl,
Just waiting for the paint to dry.

~ ~ ~ ~

"Goofy" to her nerve-whispering subordinates

Iron fisted. Middle-class gal, from out around Buffalo somewheres,

Catholic grammar school, high school,

Northwestern undergrad for pre-law,

Law and Justice at Rider, over in Jersey, law school, then back here to New York

First gig— winner winner, chicken dinner— Cuomo's staff

That's Andrew. Not old enough for Mario, but young enough for Andy boy

She might just be a Jehovah's Witness,

or a lesbian,

(as if she could love anyone other than herself)

Pulling strings— ropes— pulling ropes in Hamilton County, Herkimer, far away as Oneida and Oswego

Master Mistress of clandestine power, impenetrable deniability

Tie-in: Mother Harpo, a motorcycle bull dyke with tattoos, originally from royal money

Marian Slunge— her neé born name

That is, if she was born at all, and not hatched.

The Slunge family is Bezos rich— well, pretty close. Manufactures boxes.

Jeff B. sends you off a package, he needs a box to put it in, huh?

So, Consolidated Box and Storage

That's the Slunges

How 's zat affect Goofy?

Slunges financed every one of her campaigns,

Uses Slunge money for bribes, services, extra staff, campaign funding, lawn maintenance...

The one that's most important— campaign funding

So...?
So she's protects the Polo Rodeo
Protects their Mother
by extension, protects Zeigfried Adamsavage
Goofy will never go after the Rodeo, or Ma, or Adamsavage.
Flack like that remains off-limits, not necessary

~ ~ ~ ~

Ivy Torch

Floundering in a pool of delusion
distortion and fear clogging my ears
Shutting my eyes
Seeping ugly into my nostrils and mouth
Then,
As I manage to break the surface
To suck in some sweet lungs of rationality
for a morning at least
maybe even a day
The poet John Donne is there to greet me:
"Any man's death extinguishes me."
Annah stands by Donne's shoulder
She sees the breeze clearing my eyes, my thoughts,
and tells me a terrible tale
of "any man," who is a woman, women, black women,
destitute women, desperate women,
dying until I am required to return to my captivity.
And so I must.
I will go to the Savage of Eden
I will speak my *Nüshu* to him
Decipher my DamAx for him.
And he will release me, the killing will cease
 We are Daddy's children, Annah,
and so I must. And so I will.

~ ~ ~ ~

is shaking her head.
"No, Ivy. No. Just know."

~ ~ ~ ~

Fourth Canto: The Pursuit and Capture of Annah Torch

Zeigfried Adamsavage

Victorious I stand
My Trinidad South African boots from *Gauteng*
pressing with confidence into the quiet dust
of some shitty little road southside of White Leunge
that *gham* and *kommen* town in what they call upstate (downbeat) New York
Although yes, I do like the name
its pronunciation, if not the ambiance
White Leunge. White Lung.
Soon the world itself will be breathing
through a pair of pure, white-pumping lungs.

The world's black besmirchment irradiated forever
by the treasure about to be bestowed upon me
by our surrendering science girl.

~ ~ ~ ~

The Corner Boy

The lawyer-weasel's Subaru arrives
engine cuts out/a quick gaze around/door/weasel walk/back door opens...
Then... a little bit royally, majestically,
the little lady scientist (is it her?) de-Subarues herself,
Draped in defeat, prepared to be handed over
this her glorious commencement, the fratricidal end of normalcy
the key to DamAx-30(af) being delivered unto evil Amen.

She looks larger than Adamsavage remembers,
Stronger somehow, more confident
What a few unchained, un-raped, un-tortured weeks
will do for the complexion
He motions the lawyer/weasel to drive off, be gone, a master waving off a servant.
The Weasel concurs, never acknowledging his poignant donation to blackicide
The delivered package looking only at Adamsavage
her conquerer
The white marble Goliath who ducked her stone
Ingemar Johansson, avoiding Patterson's feeble right hook
He smiles, beckons her come forward
"No fear, no fear, fear not, sweet lady,
We shall simply sit, enjoy some tutelage together,
you shall clear up the mystery of your notes for me, for us,
and then you shall be set free. A bird. The truth shall set you free
Never to be bothered by me or the Polo Rodeo *ad nauseam*
We shall seek and find our separate eternities
Is it agreed, my gentle white lace? We agree then, yes?"

The woman speaks quietly, her words resting upon a doilied silence.

The words...

~ ~ ~ ~

Annah Torch

I am not Ivy.
I am Annah Torch.
I have come to end this.

~ ~ ~ ~

...as a heavy, ugly, black hammer appears
like a crucifix from under this woman's cloak.
So, it is the sister, not our Savior at all
and this harpy's intent?
No idea.

No need to find out, as my whistle brings the Polo Rodeo
out from the haunts of its roadside bushes
Mother Harpo, intent, purposeful, deadly
Big Mootz, oblivious as always, yet enthralled by the multiple-exploding cannon
at the end of his shooting arm
Robin the Cradle, quietly orgasmic, believing this woman-punishing
could rival child-raping in its ecstasy.
Each of the three flame-flaring their newly unwrapped
eight-inch Anacondas .44 Magnum's
which I had gifted them, along with some Macanudo knock-offs,
at our recent celebration of the return
of Our Prodigal Princess of DamAx 30.
The hand cannons provided are top-line
The cigars were cheap,
me outlaying more for fire power than papered fire.

So why were these three burly brutes positioned here in the mulberry bushes?
Because even though celebratory, I remain cautionary
All three .44's are exploding out their indiscriminate terror
And so— this less-than-avenging Avenging Angel, Annah Torch?

She bolts.

~ ~ ~ ~

I bolt.

~ ~ ~ ~

Mother Harpo

She bolts.

Having a lunatic benefactor like Adamsavage brings with it some privilege
the cigars were cheap, but these Magnums Snake Guns are divine
bulked-up Pythons, worthy of their pedigree
Unstoppable on the range.
Or in the Woods.
Or on the hunt.

As our prey bolts.

~ ~ ~ ~

She bolts.

Just like Usain— insane, but faster

Her mind subjugated (that the word I'm looking for?) more by survival than terror, she runs

to a cheap and cheesy J.C. Higgins police auction bicycle

hidden by the side of the road.

Now then, she'll ride.

~ ~ ~ ~

Mother Harpo

She's getting on a bike, boys, she's got a bicycle there!

Christ sake

To the hogs, boys, to the hogs!

No Armstrong bicycle ever made can outrun a Harley

We got ourselves a fox now,

and we be the hounds

We be the hounds
so keep shooting,

but spokes and tires only, boys

Bring 'em back alive.

~ ~ ~ ~

She bikes

Pump, Annah, pump hard them pedals,

hundred-cubic-inch Harley engines barking up your ass,

their noise scattered through muzzle-blasts of Anaconda sidearms

So pump

The riders in their leather suits and oily jeans,

are closing

Swerve right— a cramped back alley, blackened grey-grassed back yards…

Where the Rodeo is forced to dismount,

walk their hogs past garbage cans, discarded crates

As you're flying over tree roots, past backyard doghouses,

under low hanging clothes lines

The three hunters, re-mounted, holding cannons that can open up a basketball hole in your back

but they hold no capacity to think, or theorized, to make spot decisions

Every change of direction you make, every sudden move, S-shaped maneuver,

demands decision-making skills they don't got.

~ ~ ~ ~

Big Mootz

I just seen her, could be, behind the shed, along wit the mowers,
over there, head over there, I think that's her, I gotta see her,
that's her, ain't it? Maybe
Maybe it could be,
Huh?

~ ~ ~ ~

The Corner Boy

The chase transmogrifies (that a word?) from urbane to countryside,
a race, a competition of endurance and will

Your lungs are burning now, girl,
Oxygen debt
Foreclosure looming as its threat
(those hours of tri-training still paying off)
Your thigh muscles hardening into dried paste
burned into the bottom of a pan left forgotten on the stovetop for hours
Racer's Cough, nose dripping, fingers tingling, brain fogging
You gotta pee
Your crotch blood-soaked and sore,
Your brain fogging up, black clouds rolling thunder from both side panels of your eyes,
If these two side smudges meet— it's unconsciousness, delirium
Capture.

~ ~ ~ ~

Thank you, my good Cornerman, for the ointment, advice and encouragement
Got some tape? Gauze? Stitch cream? A steel plate of *No-Swell* maybe?

~ ~ ~ ~

The Corner Boy

What comes next? "Cut me, Mickey, cut me"?
Pump, Annah,
Ride
Pimpled dust blowing through your face,
mouth sucked dry by tension and exertion,
nose clogged with globs of unloosen-able snot-hogs,
bladder filled with adrenaline-sopped piss

Finally, there— it's outskirts of the Woods!
Your Woods
Those circumference trees that advertise (possibly) an escape onto safety
Continue to mash down on them pedals
Lift your ass up offa the seat— power, leverage
The taste of blood still filling your mouth
searching for any liquid at all
spittle... blood... anything...
Tongue finds only dry and caked walls of flesh
The taste of blood, easy to identify, to classify, an illusion or a phaeton of biology
The mouth blood turning into metal,
red blood cells popping like corn kernels,
your pain threshold squashed by twenty-six inch bicycle wheels,
the red blood cells giving up, turning into heme.
(Heme is iron)
This rhinitis, sopping together with dust and pollen
forming buggers of dried mucus no amount of rocket-launching can flush away
your fingers tingling,

hands engulfed by numbness
just holding onto the handgrips demands your concentration, attention
inner thighs inching, demanding fluid, lubrication

~ ~ ~ ~

Remember,

We won't be killing her yet, mates,

Not just yet

She be needed for our purposes

So shoot to maim,

Shoot to disable,

Shoot to stop the junk, not to kill

~ ~ ~ ~

The Corner Boy

You're off your bike now, Annah, hiding,
back pressed up against the cold wet halfpipe of a mud gully,
eyes locked, listening for the rumble of hogs
the ping of .44 caliber hallow-points

The mongrels have reappeared
still hounding
still shouting
firing shots into the darkened air
accompanying their bullet-heads with childish war whoops

Annah abandons the frame of her bicycle
and dives into the cold, nerve-numbing waters of Robert's Pond

~ ~ ~ ~

Mother Harpo

She's in the water now, boys

She's jumped herself in the drink, goddammit

Mootz, go round, around

Everybody, just keep smoking

She's a whale

That sweet piece of wet meat'll be ours,

we don't wanna kill her,

Adamsavage don't want her dead, huh

but don't be too too careful—

he's not here

~ ~ ~ ~

The Corner Boy

Y'know, underwater,
rocks clapped together from thirty yards away
sound like they're right tight there inside your head
That's the sound of the hollow points to Annah,
pinging by her ear
The mouth's blood taste replaced by clouded water,
just as threatening
Don't swallow, Annah, that'll pollute your system
Breathe when you can
Propel yourself, keep your ass a few inches below the surface of the Pond,
out of their sight,
out of the path of their missiles

Surface to grab a gasp of air only when you must, only when you can,
then submerge again like... like that famous submarine...
What was it?

~ ~ ~ ~

The Nautilus.

Captain Nemo. Daddy would tell us about it.

Could stay submerged, travel the entire Arctic Circle,

the entire world, never come to the surface for air or power.

~ ~ ~ ~

The Corner Boy

That's you.

Can you do that, Annah, can you last that long?

Your tongue is swelling up into a pillow,

heart pounding, irregular, inefficient,

running the risk of clotting,

calves cramping

Relax your toes, keep them pointed down

Your mouth blistering from the water corrosion

if this was salt water, your mouth'd be losing chunks of itself by now

Sea ulcers

Stroke

Capture and defeat.

~ ~ ~ ~

Annah Torch

"Dear loved ones, we are gathered here today,
for our beloved Annah.
Not defeated by the lead of bullets entering her body from the outside,
but rather from the clotting of her own blood,
attacking from within."

~ ~ ~ ~

The Corner Boy

Shit, that last zinging bullet come close,

tight, skimming the skin of your ear passing by,

but still not puncturing any flesh, am I right?

So far the zing of the bullets failing to make a hole in your foot or leg

or your callipygian (that word again?) ass

or heart

but the lead, it keeps on zinging by, don't it

~ ~ ~ ~

"Zing" must be the quickest word in the English language
Daddy used to sing us the old Judy Garland,
"Zing went the strings of my heart."

~ ~ ~ ~

Annah's senses are dulling, deprived of acumen, the pain

like a branding iron from her Dad's old cowboy movies,

totally spent, she continues to survive, to elude.

She drags herself onto the shore

like some evolution creature,

She looks around, doesn't see the pursuers

The water has given her a degree of separation.

They'll be running around the Pond to her,

barking orders no one's listening to,

shooting bullets bound to find a target

No transition tent for this triathlete

Now Annah must begin her marathon.

~ ~ ~ ~

Shit, I think I stumpled my toe.

Ouch. Ouchie.

That hurts.

Ya see any blood, I take my shoe off?

Ya seen her?

~ ~ ~ ~

The Corner Boy

Annah's mind keeps swimming, even though her body has left the water

Her vision still submerged in liquid

Her hearing clogged with mucous and moisture

Stand for a moment, Annah— just a moment, that's all we can allow ya,

Scan your land, your Woods, the *Pan-a-vision* doesn't detect present danger

until your still-clogged hearing picks up the sound of the distant choppers,

their mean rumble demanding to be fed,

bringing with them the potent sound of gunfire

Real or imagined? Thunder? You can't tell

Your mind subjugated by trauma

Not the exhaustion, you're used to that,

but by the threat, the uncertainty

These things are strangers to the state of your being.

~ ~ ~ ~

And so I revert to an earlier stage of evolution.
I run.

~ ~ ~ ~

alternating directions, changing route, skidding on and offa patted-down deer paths,

tracking the buck's direction for a few steps, a few yards,

them sidestepping into the underbrush—

that world of ticks and prickers,

 jumping stumps, leaping legs over logs, rocks

some so familiar you can remember the cracks and surface marks as you fly over.

She could become a fake-wounded robin

leadings hunters way from its nest of babies

Annah, faking a disabled path to lead the Rodeo away from Ivy.

She runs for what seems like 2:01:39 Kipchoge time

Running like some stick-thin figure of a Kenyan marathoner,

whose names always seems to rhyme with phrases like "Kip Keino,"

Covering that distance of twenty-six point two miles

Can she avoid the Wall? Heartbreak Hill?

Yeah, she can, but she's weighted down now—

by fear, fatigue, by the scant clothing still remaining on her back

With a Kenyon marathon, it's all a matter of legs and arms. And heart.

All the rest is just freight, baggage.

Annah, asks herself...

~ ~ ~ ~

Am I now ready to head back to camp, to Ivy, to Abel?
Have I eluded the baboon-brains?

~ ~ ~ ~

The Corner Boy

This off-course carries with it
the danger of leading the armed foolish army, right to her sanctum
Any final conflict wouldn't be a good one
She is exhausted, confused.

Ivy is physically, emotionally, malfunctioning and bewildered
The Hurricane lives in a natural state of simplified confusion
Yeah, the enemy is stupid, but they're armed, not weighed down by morality or ethics

The stress of her hours of running.
dizzy when she first stepped out of the water,
a drunken Venus emerging from the sea
her feet numb,
Their arteries clenched, closed

Fires need oxygen to burn, the fire in her lungs begs for air
She gasps as she runs
Her internal body temperature over one hundred-five degrees
She imagines the stress on her kidneys,
Tissue damage— gateway to organ failure
and the soreness, always the incredible soreness
of her lower back and body and legs
her toenails turned blue, then black, soon to be torn loose

~ ~ ~ ~

Screw Hemingway.

Man can be defeated *and* destroyed.

~ ~ ~ ~

Annah is stock start still, leaning up against a brick wall

She knows these bricks ain't real, they've been mind-milled by her exhaustion,

cemented by her fatigue

Recognizing this wall to be a metaphysical slab of defeat

(Defeat being a concept new to her)

Look now, she's stumbling off the wall

over to a leaning post called Total Destruction

She hears a voice calling to her, two voices,

three, and they make her feel like...

~ ~ ~ ~

...a mistake
A bee sting, a tick-bite of uncertainty
I have made a mistake.
What?

~ ~ ~ ~

The Corner Boy

She's standing up, breathing,
Trying to re-corral her mind into some kinda functioning state,
establish a plan
A plan composed of no mistakes.

She is, of course, by this time, beat to shit—
her legs sagging under the weigh of oxygen debt
Her vision swirling through blood-sopped eyes, a kid's little bloody kaleidoscope

Think, girl, think.

~ ~ ~ ~

As my noble mongrel dogs continue their pursuit,

the growling and belching of our powerful boney's engine noise,

artillery sounds

sounds of pleasure

the pleasure of unchallenged dominance

Sloshing our way through the bushes, the shrubs,

over stones, logs,

the sound of boots, tires, crushing twigs beneath our leather heels

and rimmed rubber,

growing ever closer, closer to our prey.

We have dismounted. On foot. Better? Worse?

Like their quarry, my three-deep posse is itself tiring,

but far less incapacitated by their exhaustion.

While she was furiously pumping her bike forward,

mashing down the pedals with aching legs and feet,

mine were simply twisting the hand accelerator slightly to the right

As she was submerging, then resurfacing for a quick snatch of air,

my three were standing on the shoreline,

laughing at the inaccuracy and ineffectiveness of the handguns' pot-shots

~ ~ ~ ~

Big Mootz

There, there, there she comes
She gotta get some air, right, so we clip her again then, huh?
She's no camel, right?
See them clouds? Them are her.
Lead her a little, shoot a little bit in front of her head, like I'ma doin,
I'll plunk her afore you do. Aim just a little bit in front of her front,
like me.
Like a deer, you would. You'll see. We got her now.
but try, don't just kill her first. Bring 'em back alive,
that's what Adamsavage says.

Oh, I gotta reload again.
Shit.

~ ~ ~ ~

And so, the mongrels are same time trying to puncture her with their Anacondas,
while still bringing her back alive.
Can you ascertain now how stupid these crullers must be?

Mother Harpo's just shaking her head
The playing field, it is sorta level, though
Annah's been tugged down to their level of foolishness
by body exhaustion, by exercise,
but Annah, knowing she's been making mistakes

She's come up with a plan.

~ ~ ~ ~

Annah Torch

The wounded robin. I remember.

~ ~ ~ ~

The Corner Boy

A bird, play-acting like its wing's busted,
Fluttering a path along the ground,
moving at a pace the hunters can follow,
leading them away from the nest,
away from her babies.

Away from her poisoned Ivy.

~ ~ ~ ~

A plan pockmarked with error

Did you think you could outthink me, my sweet effete American kunk?

It is I, the Savior of the Purity of the Human Race

You have allowed yourself to remain within the sphere of my danger,

within the scope and fire-range of our weapons

And I am carrying a different weapon, more logical,

Not an Anaconda handgun.

But a... a...

~ ~ ~ ~

...I'm not sure what it is he's carrying there.

Anyway, Annah's gotta sleep
She stumbles into the dampened grounds,
that ragged area where she and Hurricane Abel amass their garbage,
the stuff that won't disintegrate,
the stuff the Weasel picks up for them once a month
hauls away to the town dump.

She is asleep on garbage.

~ ~ ~ ~

Mother Harpo

Thar she blows, boys,
Shhh, quiet,
Lying on those milk cartons
We got her now
Don't kill her.
Not just yet.

But damn, that girl's quick
She's grabbing hold of a plastic bag filled with chunks of glass
probably picked up over the months along the trails
God damn it, she's on her feet now,
screaming like a banshee,
smashing the Cradle across his head, face, with the plastic sack of busted glass

The bag explodes
an atomic cloud of colored glass shards flying into the air and flesh
The Cradle screams, drops his Anaconda, grabbing at his face

Big Mootz, teary-eyed, cries, "So I gotta put her down."
As he points his front-sight muzzle at the bitch...

~ ~ ~ ~

125

... before Mootz can discharge, I fire my weapon
A meter length of thin metal barrel, muzzle and handle,
shoulder pad, telescope and trigger—
The *Dan-Inject JM Special Dart Gun—*
aimed at her fleet and fleeing ass
a thirteen millimeter pellet thunks into the white, bare thigh of the woman
She grabs at her leg, looks to the sky in confusion,
falls to the wet ground,
unconscious.

Got her.

~ ~ ~ ~

Robin the Cradle

My eyes can't see much, all that fuggen broken glass in my face
I got my jab stick, though, don't I?
I told Mootz, I said, "Let's bring us the jabbies, keep em in our saddlebags, right?"
So, me and Mootz are standin' over her now, pokin' at her,
Enjoyin' the squeals, passin' the jabbies around, hand-ta-hand.
"Mother, you wanna take a jab at the bitch?"

We just enjoyin' ourselves.
We earned it.

~ ~ ~ ~

The Corner Boy

The dart of a tranquilizer gun injects pharmaceutical dosage
into the body of its target.
Am I too technical here for ya?
Ya see, tranquilizers are acutely dependent on their dosage being correct.
If it's too much for the body size,
the target's heart, her lungs, they give out
Allergic reaction
Anaphylactic shock
Target gets dead.

But our Annah, she's six foot two, a hundred seventy pounds,
All of it sinew and muscle. A lot heftier'n the dart dosage
She's breathing
Not so much you can see unless you look close
but breathing all right
Breathing and ensnared.

~ ~ ~ ~

Fifth Canto: "This is the story of the Hurricane" (B. Dylan)

Fifth Canto: "This is the story of the Hurricane" (B. Dylan)

Admit it there, my little *bokkie*,

I have yet to murder you, yet to replace your temporal misery with everlasting peace

These many times, these past few days,

oh, the opportunity is of course mine— the means and method, the madness—

That is what your barristers call it then, over here, is it not?

Means, method... and what?

Is it madness?

No, not madness.

Opportunity.

Means, method and opportunity.

Motive! And motive!

I have them all, now, and here.

 I am shivered that I have yet to complete the act.

You Yanks with your effete courts of law. Hah.

I have assess to the tools, the weapons, the time, the space,

to end the misery of your measly life.

And yet I have not. I have yet to murder you.

Since I have no interest in you. Not ever a passing one, I'm afraid

it is your sister whom I want, need

and you, dear, are simply my conduit unto her, yeah?

~ ~ ~ ~

Just kill me.

No more of your monotoned, monotonous monologue.

Is it over yet?


~~~~
~~~~

Due time, *bokkie*, all in due time
And we do have our brownies in a snit now, do we not?
Did you think you would have me snookered by that sister-for-sister ruse?
Please
That magnificent chest of yours, not immune to puncture, is it now?
But for now, you continue to live through my benevolence

Once I chit you in for your sister, the Torch with the answers I crave,
then we shall see
but for now, you remain alive, and my dossier remains an impressive one,
anchored upon my love of mankind.
To save this world, always my Holy Grail, always has been, still is
Is that too much to ask?
To save our people?
To improve our race?
To protect us from black pollution, the sludge of mud people?

Why else it is I do everything I must do?"

~ ~ ~ ~

The Corner Boy

Adamsavage is running his fingertips along the barrel
of a *LaBomba Bean Bag Gun*
A pile of *Power Punch* cartridges at his feet,
fabric pillows of Number Nine Lead Shot,
an ounce and half of potential power,
fired at a rate of ninety meters a second,
spreading out wide during its flight to the target
(usually a human being)
 spreading out during flight, delivering an impact of a square inch,
not deadly,
not breaking the surface of the skin,
simply delivering intense pain to the target
along with some short term trauma and a more lasting, duller pain.
The victim is usually immobilized,
suffering from muscle spasms,
paralyses overwhelmed by agony

Two cartridges have been slid into the gun
Adamsavage snaps the barrel closed
He fires a round into Annah's hip.
She screams out.

~ ~ ~ ~

Annah Torch

Runs her tongue across the holes where they've pulled teeth
Spit, don't swallow
She spots a coin imbedded in the wall across the room
Ivy told her about this coin.
Ivy lost her mind, but never relented
Nor will Anna.

~ ~ ~ ~

The Corner Boy

1989, Guatemala
Sister Dianna Mae Ortiz
Roman Catholic Blessed Order of the Penguins of Ursuline
swept outta her garden by Guatemalan military thugs
bound, tortured, raped,
eventually released—
but those shit-heads kept hold of her memory,
kept her trust of humanity in a can.
She aborted the pregnancy,
along with a big chunk of her faith in God.
Polluted by survivor guilt, rest of her life
in utter words, fugged up the ass until dead
"Mine was an ordinary nightmare.
The only uncommon element—
I survived."

Annah, bound, can see the form of Sister Dianna
hiding there in the shatters,
Huddled there, along with her Ivy.

~ ~ ~ ~

Maria Del Cechio

Mister Weasel Lawyer man,

I am a poor woman,

I come to you for help.

My daughter, some monsters, they kill her.

My family, we take out a borrow loan from the bank.

To bury her. To the undertaker. To wash the paint from her body.

Not enough. *Dinero*, you see? We go to the local man on street there,

to get the rest.

That's okay, fine.

The wake, the funeral, bury, sweet God of mine

But the *policía*, they do nothing, see?

They no find the animals kill my baby.

They no say it, but they thinking,

"Just a whore, just nother Columbia whore."

You help me, I come to you.

Por favor. Por el amor de Dios. Por mia Gina.

~ ~ ~ ~

136

Mrs. Del Checio,

I have been dealing with these people for many years.

Through many deaths

I too— this you might not know—

I too have one I love, one who has been taken from me,

in danger of being murdered

Just as your sweet daughter was murdered.

And for me, me too, the authorities, they do nothing

They say to you that your daughter was nothing

They tell me the same

The woman I speak of,

they tell me— no papers, no missing person reports, nothing

to them, she does not exist. They prefer this absence of existence

just as your daughter, your sweet one, she did not exist

So they say.

But your Gina lived. She was.

And this woman I speak of.

She lives.

She is.

~ ~ ~ ~

Entombed in paralysis

Him and pal Protski, good cops shackled and chained by forces beyond

"What Goofy wants, Goofy gets

She never gets tired, and she never regrets."

District Attorney Sarah T. Guffleberg

"But, Madam D.A., a woman's been snatched, is being held.

We think we know who, we might even know where."

"Sit on it, boys, she's not our traction. She's a hermit, lives in the Woods.

She does not exist."

Gumm, tweed sports jacket over Hawaiian shirt with World War II bombers,

shrugs at his pal, Leo Protski, special investigator, the office of Goofy.

Both shrug out their "Waddaya gonna do's?" to each other

The bodies of the two cops, an apple sitting beside a pencil

"Ya can't fight City, Small, can we?"

Both men respect the Weasel, as a defense attorney, he plays things straight

Justice for his client, not absolution

He came to them asking about his former employee, the missing forest babe

Wish they could help

reminding themselves not to call him Weasel in front of the press

Gumm has been a shooting gallery target

since the first oil-base paint coated body was discovered

Now, this.

He steps up, delivers his boilerplate with gravity and calmness:

"The White Leunge Police Department shall continue to hold

the well being and safety of all of its citizens
In the highest regard.
We shall continue to…"

~ ~ ~ ~

My sacred Annah,

I feel wisps of your soft hair falling across my face

floating from that focused inch above me

your eyes smiling down

my lips coating you with gentle adoration

Our two selves held close as

God's fingertips

My hand reaching between your legs from behind

to caress you there

Even within this total darkness

your beauty glows

I see it perfectly

Emitting its own ferocious light.

Such is my fantasy.

~ ~ ~ ~

The Corner Boy

So you're asking– the Weasel, ya think he been getting any?

Well, his wang and Annah's vaj *have* shared the same space

and maybe the same thoughts even,

but never at the same time.

Trains and tunnels, ships and ports,

pudendas of passion,

but no symbiosis

Is that the word?

Anyway, that's the flux and fucks of the world.

~ ~ ~ ~

All religions have a Holy Fool, one outsider who sees the truth

Jesus, Mohammad, Buddha, Tony Roberts.

Such is the Hurricane.

He lives among the muskrats, the honey badgers

with a single friend. And she has been taken from him.

The new sister, Ivy, she's not of any use, she simply sits, stares at the trees

So the Hurricane has come to the lawsuit's office

where he does not remember wallpaper

The lawsuit's chair is soft— stuffed with leaves? Grass? Moss?

The Hurricane hopes he remembers how to say words

Animals can understand without talking

The trees speak, but mostly to each other

The birds sing— but songs of warning, of war, battle, threats

Lawsuits they talk, that is all they do

"Annah is your fried, Abel. And you're worried about her. I understand."

"I broke my leg, was coughing blood from my eyes, my ears. She takes care of me."

"A friend. Mine too."

"Where she at, sir?"

The lawsuit is smiling at the Hurricane—a coyote showing teeth?

The lawsuit is pushing a bowl of beans toward him

Candy beans of many different colors. The Hurricane remembers such beans

The lawsuit is talking, but there are too many words

"Where she be, sir?"

"The police think they know. We suspect, but we can't do..."

"Where she at?"

The lawsuit repeats a name.

The Hurricane tries to sound out the name hard, solid,
but it carries with it a question mark

"Pump House?"

~ ~ ~ ~

wipes his captive's blood from his hands as he remembers...

"Our country was a magical place back then, my blokes

The air filled with song, surrounded by color. Smiles of content."

He snorts back some black mucus.

"*Mi Da* was a dentist. He, Mum, Jessie— they all died in Sharpeville, down near Johannesburg."

The black rioting of 1984

Reports that all fourteen deaths involved were black citizens proved to be incorrect.

"*Mi Da* was driving us to our boat."

A missed turn, into the very jaws of the riot

"We were dosed in gasoline siphoned from an abandoned fuel truck.

Me da, stunned by panic, driving us to safety, instead exploded us into flames."

Crumpled the car into a stoplight stanchion.

"I was found sucking at my toes in a swamped culvert."

Burns on the hips and stomach are still painful if he cinches his belt too tightly.

Adamsavage uses the back of his hand to wipe Annah's blood from his forehead.

"It is for us, the living, to carry on to that for which they died."

The eradication of the black bastard race.

"Our Father, who art in heaven. Probably."

The strong, silent white woman, lashed to a pole in the next room.

Killing her would be difficult.

"But if we must..."

~ ~ ~ ~

is a man once driven into the street by a Job-like series of marital/business failures
leading to a *smörgasbord* of chemical addiction
Headed into the Woods, for just a one-night stand
Took him two years to realize the Woods had boiled all his additions down to one:
the woman who saved him.

She had found him spit-coughing and mumbling,
wrapped in a green tarp. On the mythical border of Topher's Woods,
his brown skin flaking away with each caress of breeze
blood mixed with phlegm dripping from his nose, blood-pus from both ears
the whites of his eyes smeared with red, glazed over in panic

Her first words to him: "I will not hurt you."

The woman cared for him, nursed him, comforted him,
washed away his dirt, bathed his wounds,
Poured out a dark amber liquid
that turned the melon-shaped bundles of fat, wiggling white parasites
his ass had been expelling
back into a welcomed, softer shit.
Few words were spoken between them,
the desire to voice slowly drying up, shriveling to next-to-nothing
The paucity of words a healing, like a healing of wounds.

Now, she had been taken from him.
Someone is hurting her, just like he had been hurt

“They will not hurt you.”

~ ~ ~ ~

Big Mootz

All mornings, either side of three o'clock,
empty of mind, full of bladder,
it's off to the thunder box
Then, relieved and breathing heavy, back in bed,
tugging pudd with thoughts of Sassie
Best dog ever.

Can't sleep,
Up now and playing with his cartridges
Hornady XTP's
.44 Mag 240 gr XTP– Extreme Terminal Performance shells
Lining them up, marching the little golden cylinders across the tabletop
little soldiers
Muzzle velocity, energy,
plus discipline
Back in bed with a tired pudd and wondering mind
(What's the word for *cabbage*?)
A clatter next door– What was that?
Did I remember to strap the bitch down? Better go see.

Mootz slips the .44 mags back into the Anaconda, where they belong
His flap palm opens the door where they've been keeping the jungle bitch...

~ ~ ~ ~

"Good morning, Mootz,
How are *you*?"

~ ~ ~ ~

Big Mootz

as a kid, always hated getting in trouble
wetting the bed, killing a kitten
grew up big ,with the speed of a hard-on at a whore house,
but never lost his fear of getting in trouble
Ma, that first Ma, she'd use a golf club on him. Driver wood.

He's in trouble now.
The jungle bitch's somehow got loose, is standing there
with some big black guy Mootz don't know. What the–?
The Anaconda from its holster– speed and panic–
but the .44 Hornady shell hits a wall
The Anaconda's kickback, greatest feeling there is,
but Mootz can't enjoy it– too much else going on
The blackie jumps in front of the bitch,
black ass moving faster than a speedy bullet.
The black face gets punctured with a small, red hole, just off center of one of the eyes,
the back of blackie's head explodes onto the face of the captive bitch
a face held stunned, covered with bits of the blackie's blood and bone and brain
She's throwing something–garden pliers
She's strong, stronger than the sister with the crinkly bones was,
and skilled, because the pliers are sticking out of Mootz's crotch.
He's gotta laugh. The pliers make it look like he's got a hard-on.
"We used to cell em boners."
So, two boners in one night. Not bad.
Mootz's laughing vision of the room is set behind seven thin black bars
crossing horizontally across his eyes,

The bars fatten themselves into each other, and then into full black
Big Mootz feels— feels because he can't see— the room tipping up, going lopsided,
Until a slab of cold, flat cement crushes its way into Mootz's face.

~ ~ ~ ~

The Corner Boy

Annah figures a mirror is something robs you of your modesty,

of any honest well-awareness

so instead, she's back in her Woods, leaning over the shallow and still water

of the Pollywog Pond

Looking down

Studying her appearance. And her options.

Remnants from the Hurricane speckle the skin of her face

There is no authority other than that of God and nature

The polluted world holds only the fakery and deception of a fathom system of law

Particles of Hurricane smeared across her face like a road map,

a guide to what needs to be done. Where it is she must go

The blood is the most obvious cosmetic, turned brown by the days

Those darker shades must be brain chunks, colored like day-old bread

A little lighter there— skull

Them lines of black, looking like her own lip cracks and eye lashes,

they're the hair of a black man.

Annah closes her eyes and listens to the sweet, swift battlecry of the birds

She looks to heaven, cups pond water in both hands

No.

The water drips back down through her fingers.

The Hurricane's blood splatter will remain upon her face

Or is it "blood spatter"? Them are both words.

But either way, the Hurricane's blood stays on her face,

Until...

~ ~ ~ ~

Annah Torch

Until I kill them all.

~ ~ ~ ~

Sixth Canto: Venge

This morning, my sweet Annah,

the Savage came by here

Trying to use me to find you

Trying to use you to find Ivy

Trying to use Ivy to find immortality.

To find his genocide.

I found out the Posse's off to Boston for some rest and rehab

Offered me Boston Garden tix

(Yeah, I still call it that)

They'll be raising Kevin Garnet's number to the ceiling

The whole Rodeo will be there.

Me, I'll be staying home.

~ ~ ~ ~

Annah Torch

I hate crowds.
Collective inconsequence.

~ ~ ~ ~

TD Garden

Section: Floor 18

Row: BB

Seat: 16

Zeigfried Adamsavage clicks open his phone.

Picture of the Cradle

sitting in a toilet stall

Loge Bathroom Number 4

Pants to his ankles

Startled look in his eyes

The rounded dome of a ball peen hammer

imbedded in his forehead.

Not a selfie.

~ ~ ~ ~

Big Mootz

My crotch still stingin from them fuggen garden pliers
Savage sends me to go check on the Cradle in the crapper
Maybe musta fell in.
Tells me to Hey, watch myself.
What for?

In the first shitter, one down from the hotdogs,
a stall door— locked from the inside
Um shakin it, bangin,
If he's in there, he ain't correspondin
A note on the wall:
"Hub Exit B."

~ ~ ~ ~

Same TD Garden section and seat, second ping, second pic
Snapped by Cradle's phone, shot from above:
Big Mootz, flopped on his back, inside a Dumpster
Can tell it's Mootz by the belly.
His face is gone,
hammered beyond recognition,
beyond compassion
beyond comprehension.

~ ~ ~ ~

Zeigfried Adamsavage

Hey listen now, Mother, there's something going on here,

but I don't know what it is, do I, Mr. Jones?

Either way, we are out.

We'll have to see the black gorilla's number fly some other time

It's a silly game anyway

Full-grown Negroes running around in short pants

The both of us both prefer the Cricket then, do we not?

This is certainly the work of the jungle bitch.

~ ~ ~ ~

Mother Harpo

Dropped and dying, out on the tar of Lovejoy Place

cross street from the Garden

Her Anaconda beside her on the cold, wet pavement

Close by... but not God's fingertips to Adam's

Abandoned by her recently absconded boss

Adamsavage: "Mother, we'll both do better split up, let's go."

Fucker.

The beautiful Torched and venging angel, legs straddling Mother from above

Mother's thought:

Goddamit, even with all the blood, it is a beautiful face.

Mother's penultimate statement:

"You'll never find him.

He's gone deep,

Gone from the Pump House."

Her final words:

"An abandoned A-frame on Verbeck,

in Schaghticoke.

Over by the fairgrounds.

Go get him, he's a turd."

~ ~ ~ ~

160

That woman really did look like Harpo Marx
With all the curly white hair and everything.

~ ~ ~ ~

Zeigfried Adamsavage

With a *Mannlicher-Carcano* infantry carbine,

the very weapon that extinguished, beheaded, your beloved president/playboy.

Perhaps the American press will appreciate the subtlety,

Although American appreciation of history is capricious at best.

Plus a jolly-top anachronism— the Vortex Viper scope

simply by drilling a few new screw holes.

With patience, planning, and the proper equipment,

ballistic turrets, and zero stops,

any of us can become a sniper.

In my crosshairs— the Torch woman

Did you really think I wouldn't plan for your tracking me down?

After you annihilating my Polo Rodeo in those singular, disturbing ways?

So I find myself in the shooter's prone position:

Belly pressed to dirt, legs spread, right knee bent, left leg parallel to the spine,

elbows placed solid, shoulders level.

Relaxed. Eye on the front sight, not on the woman.

Am I being impulsive?

Certainly. I should simply be waiting. Live bait attracts better than the dead.

But impulsive or not, vengeance trumps all

As you step forward— my scoped queen, my dragon, my Hera

I press the plump pad of my finger onto the trigger mechanism

take in a full deep breath, release ten percent of it,

and gently squee...

~ ~ ~ ~

Ivy Torch

When eleven, I stung a wren with my Wham-O,
Stunned and fluttering, a red blood ring surrounding its tiny left eye
Daddy and Annah paced it in a basket of straw,
tried to feed it with an eyedropper.
By the morning, it had died.

I vowed to never again kill a living thing.
And I have honored that vow.

Until now.

My backbone finally found,
and it was sturdy.

~ ~ ~ ~

The Corner Boy:

And so's, we find Annah Torch kneeling in the soft sand by the Polliwog Pond
She cups her hands, brings the Baptismal waters up to her face,
The blood of Hurricane Abel to be finally washed away.
"As we forgive those who trespass against us..."
Well, "forgive" might be a bit of a spin. Since she hammered them to death
"And deliver us from evil..."
You mean "de-liver" as in "to remove the liver organ from a recent corpse"?

~ ~ ~ ~

Annah Torch

"Vengeance is fine, saith the Lord." *Romans 12:19*
Was merely a coptic misprint that changed the word to "mine."

Thanks for the buggy ride, Coroner Boy

~ ~ ~ ~

Spoken like a true Christian.

Anyway, what's that the Caulfield kid said?
"Don't go start talking about people,
You'll only start missing them."

You ready for another beer?
Hey, Jerry, over here!

~ ~ ~ ~

~ ~ ~ ~